Mudcat Kids

WHEN PIGS GO BAD

SUSAN E. MERRITT

Illustrated by Andy Cienik

Vanwell Publishing Limited

St. Catharines, Ontario

Design: Linda Moroz
Editor: Angela Dobler

Vanwell Publishing Limited
1 Northrup Crescent
P.O. Box 2131
St. Catharines, Ontario L2R 7S2

Printed in Canada

04   03   02   01   00   99   6   5   4   3   2   1

Canadian Cataloguing in Publication Data

Merritt, Susan E.
    When pigs go bad

(Mudcat kids)
ISBN 1-55125-027-6

I. Cienik, Andy. II. Title. III. Series

PS8576.E748W43 1999   jC813'.54   C99-932119-6
PZ7.M47Wh 1999

ISSN: 1482-7638

Contents

1. Mean as a Junkyard Dog 1

2. BOOM-baba-BOOM 5

3. Whatever It Is, It's Bad 9

4. Bears are Scary 15

5. But a Pig Looks You
   Straight in the Eye 21

6. And Don't Make a Fuss . . . 26

7. The Hardest Part of
   Doing Nothing 34

8. Running For Her Life 42

9. This Story Has Legs 47

10. It's So Crazy 54

CHAPTER ONE

Mean as a Junkyard Dog

Jeannie Sawchuk raced around the corner of J.J. Metcalf School. Her sweaty T-shirt stuck to her back.

"Yay, Jeannie!" shouted Zora Parks from the playground. Monica Lamont stood beside her under the trees. "Why don't you stop Jeannie?" shouted Monica. "You've already done ten laps around the playground."

Jeannie shook her head and kept running. "Must," she gasped out as she ran past, "do two more."

"Jeannie sure practises a lot," said Zora. She gingerly ran her tongue over her braces. Dr. Tanaka had tightened them that morning and now her teeth were sore. "She's been running every day like this for weeks. No one else on the Mudcat track team works this hard."

Monica nodded. "Jeannie really wants to win on Field Day."

"Everyone expects you to win when you're on the track team," said Zora. She made a face. "Especially Coach Winston."

When Jeannie finally returned, Zora handed her a towel and a water bottle. Jeannie took a long drink. "Ahhhhhh, that feels better," she gasped.

She wiped her face with the towel and re-tightened the elastic bands on her braids. Still panting, she walked slowly back and forth in the shade.

Monica pointed at a figure marching across the playground toward them.

"Not Blabitha," groaned Jeannie. Tabitha Butterfield was a year older, and mean as a junkyard dog. She was a blabbermouth, and a tattle-tale too.

Blabitha stopped in front of the three girls, with her usual sly smile.

"Hey Monica, are those your mother's drapes you're wearing?" she asked.

Monica looked down in dismay at her flowered top. She *had* thought it was pretty, but Blabitha's words made her feel unsure.

"Leave her alone!" said Zora.

"Yeah, and how are ya gonna make me, Brace Face?" Blabitha shot back.

"Cut it out, Tabitha," said Jeannie, still wiping sweat from her red face. "What are you doing over here, anyway?"

"Nothing. I'm just on my way to see the cool kids — you know, *my* friends? I wouldn't be caught dead hanging out with a bunch of losers like you." She laughed and started to stroll away. Over her shoulder she shouted back, "And it's no use practising, Sawchuk. I can beat you at any race, any time. And you know it!"

Jeannie, almost shaking with rage, wondered for the hundredth time why so many kids thought Blabitha was cool. Maybe it was because Blabitha was annoyingly good at all sports. Maybe it was because she had such a mean mouth.

Jeannie imagined herself beating Blabitha in a race, and instantly felt better.

"How come Blabitha doesn't have to do laps at lunch recess? Isn't she on the track team too?" asked Monica.

Jeannie shrugged. "She always sucks up to Coach Winston, so he lets her off. And Blabitha thinks she's so good that she doesn't need to practise like the rest of us."

"Is she really that good?" asked Zora.

"She's pretty good at most races," Jeannie had to admit. "But I think I can beat her in the 800-metre race." She looked over at Blabitha's little group. "Someone has to take her down a notch or two," she folded her arms across her chest, "and I'd like that someone to be me." Jeannie continued, *"That's* why I'm practising so hard for Field Day!"

CHAPTER TWO

BOOM·baba·BOOM

Still glaring at Blabitha and her cool friends, Jeannie took another long drink from her water bottle. Then she pulled Super Pig out of her backpack. Jeannie had a large collection of stuffed animals and often brought Super Pig, her favourite, to school.

Most of the Mudcat kids brought in stuff to put on their desks. Monica brought in plastic trolls with long, weirdly colored hair. Zora brought in winged horses. Some of the boys in Jeannie's class appeared with minia-ture cars or muscle-popping monsters.

Jeannie gave Super Pig a quick hug. Super Pig was round and pink and soft. She had a large, friendly smile and her short, sturdy legs ended in V-shaped hooves.

When Jeannie first got Super Pig, Rudy claimed the toy was part Vulcan. Rudy was Jeannie's older brother. He was a huge fan of

Star Trek and knew every TV episode by heart. Whenever his parents asked where he was going with the car, he would always say, "To boldly go, where no man has gone before."

"Hey, Jeannie, this pig's giving the Vulcan Salute," Rudy had said, "Like when Mr. Spock says 'Live long and prosper'." Rudy held his hand up with his fingers spread in a V-shape.

Rudy had wanted Jeannie to name the toy pig "Spock," but Jeannie had refused. Instead, she tied a small, black cape around the pig's neck and called her "Super Pig." But Jeannie agreed that Super Pig had large, pointy Vulcan ears, like Mr. Spock.

There was a loud squawk overhead. The girls looked up to see three gulls circling over the playground. When one of Blabitha's friends tossed a broken cookie onto the grass, the gulls dropped from the sky. The quickest one pounced on the cookie with shrill cries of joy.

"Look at those gulls fighting over food," said Zora. "I wish they'd stay at the lake."

The first gull gulped the cookie down. With wings slightly spread, the other two gulls hopped around in the grass, searching for tasty bits of garbage.

"They sure are bold," agreed Jeannie. "And they're hard to chase away."

"Just like Blabitha!" laughed Zora.

BOOM-baba-BOOM-baba-BOOM. They all felt the noise a split second before they heard it. Then the girls saw the beat-up car cruising down Main Street. Its windows were rolled down and the four teenage boys inside had turned the car stereo on full blast. A skull-shattering BOOM-baba-BOOM-baba-BOOM poured out into the soft spring air.

Warily the kids on the playground watched the car BOOM-baba-BOOM past their school. Every Mudcat kid believed that teenagers were big and scary and mean.

"What kind of music is that?" shouted Monica above the noise. Jeannie knew all about loud music. "It's heavy metal," she shouted back. Rudy had a lot of heavy metal tapes at home.

"It's scaring the gulls," Monica shouted. "Look!"

The big birds, shocked by the throbbing, violent sound of the music, took off in a flurry of white. It was weird, Jeannie thought as she watched, that just a loud noise could frighten away such bold, hungry creatures.

The gulls circled the school once, then headed back to the lake, complaining bitterly along the way.

CHAPTER THREE

Whatever It Is, It's Bad

Jeannie, Zora and Monica had chosen "The Mighty Oak Tree" as their group science project. The next Saturday they rode their bikes out to the Olafson farm to look at some huge old trees. Jeannie's grandmother, Mrs. Olafson, had a farm just outside of Williamsville with a large oak wood.

The first time Monica and Zora had visited the farm they were surprised. They had imagined a white, wooden farmhouse, with lilacs around its big front porch. Instead, the Olafson farmhouse was a small, oddly-shaped house set far back from the road. One side of the house was nothing but a huge wall of glass. Jeannie had explained that in winter, the sun pouring through the glass heated the house so well that her grandmother didn't need a furnace.

Mrs. Olafson, who was always known as "Granny O," was outside when the girls arrived. The classical music she loved was playing softly on her portable cassette player in the garden.

She was a slim, quick-moving woman who greeted each girl with a smile and a hug. "I was just getting ready to pick my lettuce," she said. "But first, girls, come in for a snack." Granny O dusted off her jeans and led the girls into the house.

The girls took off their bike helmets and backpacks and enjoyed munching cookies at Granny O's big kitchen table. Jeannie passed around her brother's *Insults for All Occasions* book. The girls laughed as they took turns reading insults out loud.

"Do you think memorizing these will really help us with Blabitha?" asked Zora.

"Can't hurt," replied Jeannie with a mouthful of crumbs. She narrowed her eyes. "Next time Blabitha opens that mean mouth of hers, we'll be ready!"

When all the cookies were gone, Jeannie, Monica and Zora unpacked their travelling friends. They carefully arranged Super Pig, several purple-haired trolls and a yellow winged horse on a wicker sofa in a bright patch of sun.

"We thought we'd gather some acorns for our project, Granny O," said Jeannie.

"And I brought this along to take a picture of the Olafson Oak," said Monica, pulling a small camera out of her backpack.

The Olafson Oak was a huge tree, almost four hundred years old. It stood in the centre of the woods and must have been a big tree even when the pioneers arrived. Monica thought it would be nice to put a picture of the giant tree on the cover of their project.

Granny O nodded. "Good idea," she said, picking up a basket. "This year I put my vegetable garden near the oak wood. Come on girls, on the way over, I'll show you my new crop of lettuce."

They walked past Granny O's chickens scratching in the dirt and past the farm pond where Granny O's geese swam around in lazy circles.

"There's no posts or wire fencing for love or money around here this year," said Granny O, as they tramped along. "Those big floods on the other side of the country took out a lot of fences. I can't put a fence around my new vegetable garden for a while because everything's been trucked off to the flood area. But I'm eager to taste my first lettuce—" Granny O stopped and stared.

"What on earth—" She looked at her garden in stunned silence.

The girls also stared. All they could see

was a few chewed-up lettuce plants and a lot of churned-up dirt.

"My lettuce!" gasped Granny O. "It's almost all gone! Something's been raiding my garden!" she sputtered. She bent over and studied the ground for tracks.

"Raccoons?" suggested Monica.

"It's not raccoon tracks," muttered Granny O.

"Deer?" asked Jeannie.

"No, these aren't deer tracks. This animal has four toes, and deer have two."

"Then, what is it?" asked Zora.

Puzzled, Granny O shook her head. "These tracks are familiar, but I can't think what wild animal would make them. It's not a deer. Yet it has cloven hooves like a deer. See?"

The girls crowded around and stared at the marks in the soil. "You mean, that sort of V-shape?" Zora asked.

Granny O nodded, then frowned at her ruined garden. "Well, whatever it is, it's bad."

Granny O looked at the girls. "You know, there is one way to find out." She raised her eyebrows. "Lately I've been hearing a lot of talk about 'Girl Power.' How would you girls like to use your own 'Girl Power'?"

"What," asked Jeannie cautiously, "do you want us to do?"

"I want you to become detectives," said Granny O. "And I pay fair wages," she added, "in the form of homemade pie."

CHAPTER FOUR

Bears are Scary

"It's getting cold out here," said Monica, later that afternoon. She zipped up her jacket.

The bright spring sun was about to set and a chill was creeping across the meadow that lay between the girls and the woods. Their picnic blanket was beginning to feel cold and damp.

"At least, we found some acorns," said Zora.

"And I can get the film developed right away," said Monica. "Then we can scan the best picture of the Olafson Oak into the computer and print it on our cover page."

Zora nodded. "My cousin Hassiba just became a newspaper reporter. She takes photos and does that sort of thing all the time."

"It's getting dark," said Jeannie, dropping her voice. "Whatever is raiding

Granny O's garden will probably show up at dusk for the rest of the lettuce. That's right about now."

The three girls huddled together and Jeannie spread one of Granny O's wool blankets over their legs.

They peered intently at the edge of the woods. A ribbon of Canada geese flew over their heads toward the lake. A cardinal sang its "I'm red! I'm red! It's neeeeeat!" song, then fell silent.

Suddenly Zora spotted something. She nudged Jeannie and Monica, then pointed. A bush on the edge of the woods moved slightly. The girls peered at the spot in the growing darkness.

Jeannie felt her heart begin to pound. What if it was something dangerous, like a bear? She had never heard of any bears in the area, but still....

"I see it now," whispered Monica. "Look!" A shape had appeared in the meadow.

"The bush is moving again," whispered Jeannie. "Whatever it is, there must be two of them." Now her heart was really pounding. Could they outrun bears? she wondered.

Zora sucked in her breath. "I know what they are!" Zora whispered excitedly. "They're pigs!"

Jeannie sighed with relief. Bears were scary. Pigs were not.

"It's a mother pig and a piglet," said Monica. "Look."

"Coooool," breathed Zora.

Jeannie saw a dirty grey pig with a small pig behind it, trotting across the meadow toward Granny O's vegetable garden.

This little pig went to market. And this little pig stayed home! Jeannie laughed at the thought.

The pigs stopped at the sound of her laugh and stared in their direction. Then they continued toward the garden.

"Hey, that's Granny O's garden. Shoo you pigs! Go away now!" Jeannie jumped up and waved her arms. The mother pig looked over, then stuck her snout in the soil and began to root around. The piglet hid behind its mother.

"Oh, Jeannie, leave them alone," said Zora. "They're cute!"

"They're cute, but look at the mess they're making of my granny's garden. They can go and make a mess somewhere else."

"Oh, listen to them talking to each other," said Monica. They could hear the pigs grunting back and forth.

Jeannie pulled an old tennis ball out of her jacket pocket. "I'm going to throw this at the mother pig."

"You aren't going to hurt her, are you?" asked Monica anxiously.

"Naw. I'll just throw it near her. It won't

hit her. It'll just scare them away."

Jeannie took a couple of steps and hurled the ball. The mother pig stopped rooting around long enough to watch the ball fall near her with a plop. She lifted her head and stared at Jeannie for several seconds, then shoved her snout back into the soil. The little pig stayed close to its mother.

The mother pig's bold stare made all three girls suddenly nervous. The animal had a strange, wild look about her.

Monica remembered the stories of King Arthur and the Knights of the Round Table. Didn't they sometimes hunt wild boar? And wasn't a wild boar really a wild pig? And didn't some of the knights get killed by wild boars?

"Uh, Jeannie," Monica called after her, "I think this pig might be kinda wild. Why don't we just leave. We can tell Granny O about the pigs and see what she says."

"Awww?" protested Zora. Although cold and damp, she wanted to stay and watch the pigs some more. This was 'way more interesting than working on "The Mighty Oak Tree."

But Jeannie had to agree with Monica. The mother pig had a fierce look in her eyes, Jeannie thought. She was definitely not the sweet little pig from the movie *Babe*. And she was definitely not the sweet little pig from *Charlotte's Web*. And besides, it was getting dark now. She walked quickly back to her friends.

"Look! The stars are coming out," murmured Monica. "They're so much brighter in the country."

"Yeah," said Zora. She pointed up above their heads. "Know what constellation that is?"

"No, what?" asked Jeannie.

"The *pig* dipper!" Zora replied.

They all groaned.

"Hey, don't you know pig jokes are *boar*-ing?" Monica demanded. Then she grinned.

Still groaning and laughing, the girls slipped back to Granny O's to feast on home-made apple pie.

CHAPTER FIVE

But A Pig Looks You Straight in the Eye

"Pigs!" said Granny O with a frown. "They must have escaped from somewhere. But none of the farms around here keep pigs."

"Maybe the pigs escaped from a slaughterhouse," suggested Zora. "There's one near Hopedale."

"Or maybe the pig escaped from a truck on her way to the slaughterhouse. Then she gave birth in the woods and only one piglet survived," suggested Jeannie.

"Either way," said Monica, "she's a brave pig!"

Granny O smiled. "My grandfather used to keep pigs. Said they were better than a watchdog. 'Cause they're smart, you know.

Smarter than horses. Maybe even smarter than dogs! My grandpa used to say, 'A cat looks down on you. A dog looks up to you. But a pig looks you straight in the eye'!"

She frowned again. "But what am I going to do? They're not toys like Super Pig. They're real! And they'll eat up all my crops. I sell my vegetables to pay the bills."

"Maybe you could catch the pigs and keep them in a pen," suggested Jeannie. She loved her grandmother's place but thought it needed more animals.

"Any of you girls ever tried to catch a pig?" asked Granny O.

The girls shook their heads.

"Well, they can run like the wind. Whoever came up with the saying 'lazy as a pig' has never tried to catch one. Even if you're fast enough to grab a running pig, there's no fur and not much hair to hold onto. They slip out of your hands like butter.

"Besides," she continued, "it sounds like these pigs have gone wild. They won't just give up their freedom. The mother pig will put up a real fight."

Then Granny O shook her head. "Of course there won't be a pig problem for long. Once word gets out that there are wild pigs in the oak wood, every idiot with a gun will be sneaking out here to take a shot. They'll ignore my 'No Hunting' signs and shoot everything in sight. I worry about the rest of the wildlife in those woods — and about the stray bullets when they miss."

Monica swallowed her last bite of apple pie. "So let's not tell anyone about the pigs. It'll be our secret."

Jeannie looked at her grandmother. "We won't tell anyone, Granny O. We can all keep a secret."

"Then the pigs won't get killed," pleaded Zora. It didn't seem fair to hunt down a pig that had been brave enough and clever enough to escape from a slaughterhouse.

"But what about my garden? I can't just sit back and watch my crops get gobbled up by pigs. Even cute ones."

"What if we think of a way to keep them out of your garden?" asked Jeannie. "*Then* could the pigs stay?"

"Yes," said Granny O. "I'm letting most of my land turn back into forest, anyway." She thought for a minute. "As long as the pigs keep out of my garden they can live in the woods. But my next crop of lettuce will be ready to plant outside in a week. So, you have one week to come up with a plan."

She shook her head. "Otherwise, I'll have

to get a hunter to do the job. If the pigs have to be killed, I'd rather have someone who will do it properly. That way the animals won't suffer and the rest of the wildlife won't get shot."

The three girls looked at each other and nodded. "We can come up with a plan, Granny O, you'll see," said Jeannie. "We'll use our Girl Power!"

"And we won't tell a soul about the pigs," added Zora.

"Promise," Monica chimed in. "Let's pinky swear!"

The three girls locked baby fingers with each other and said solemnly, "Tell no one about the pigs. Pinky swear!"

"Now put your bikes in the back of my truck and I'll drive you all home," said Granny O.

She raised her eyebrows. "But your plan to save the pigs better be a good one!"

CHAPTER SIX

And Don't Make a Fuss

"What do you mean I can't run in the race?" demanded Jeannie. She stared in disbelief at Coach Winston, leaning against the gym's double doors. Painted on the wall above his head was the school motto, "Anything is paw-sible."

Coach Winston was the hairiest man the Mudcat kids had ever seen.

He had thick dark hair on his long arms and on the tree trunk legs that stuck out of his gym shorts. He had hair growing out of his nostrils and hair growing out of his ears. Large tufts of hair even popped up out of the buttoned-up collars of the golf shirts that Coach Winston wore every day. Behind his back, the kids called him Winston the Wookie.

Now Coach Winston shrugged and would not look her in the eyes. Instead, he stared down the school hallway. "Uh, now Jeannie." He began to fiddle with his silver whistle. "I was pretty sure that this year the Track and Field Association would bring in an 800-metre race for girls. So I had you train for it. But, uh, they didn't. The only 800-metre race is for boys."

"But why?" said Jeannie.

"Uh, well, I guess girls your age aren't strong enough for such a long race. It's about half a mile."

"But *boys* my age are?" Jeannie demanded. She couldn't believe what she was hearing.

"The Track and Field Association in Hopedale makes the rules," he said, shifting from foot to foot, "not me." His running shoes, the size of Tonka trucks, squeaked with every move.

"But, Coach I can run that distance. And I've been training for weeks!"

"Well, uh, dear, you can do the 400-metre dash, instead. That's the longest race we have for girls. And," he added, "the top two girls in the 400-metre will go on to represent J.J. Metcalf in the regional finals."

"And the top two in the 800-metre?" Jeannie asked.

"The top two *boys*," Coach Winston said firmly, "will go on to the finals as well."

"But why didn't you tell me this earlier, Coach? I would have trained differently for the 400. That's only a sprint." Jeannie fought back tears of anger.

"Well we can't argue with the rules, now, can we?" he said blandly. "Just be a good girl and don't make a fuss. You've still got the 400."

He paused. "Uh, I think I hear my phone ringing." Shoes squeaking, Coach Winston escaped into the gym.

Some coach, Jeannie thought bitterly. He probably *is* part wookie. Or part susquatch. And too lazy to check the race rules until today. She had counted on beating Blabitha in the 800. But she wasn't so sure about winning the 400. Blabitha was pretty good at that distance.

And then, on top of everything else, to be told that girls were weaker than boys!

Over lunch, Monica and Zora agreed. "It's not fair," said Zora. "But it's no big surprise. Everyone knows that Winston doesn't like

girls much. If a girl puts her hand up to answer in class, he never picks her."

"Did you go to the office and check out the rules?" asked Monica. "Maybe he's just making it up."

"No, I checked," Jeannie said miserably. "The race rules haven't been changed in years. They say the top two *boys* in the 800-metre will be sent on to the regional finals." She made a face. "I sure hate to be told I'm not as good as a boy."

"It's stupid," protested Monica, "You're the fastest long-distance runner in the school."

"Yeah, why would girls be too weak to run that far?" said Zora. "That's so lame." She picked a piece of apple out of her braces. "Look at the mother pig. I bet she ran really fast to escape from the slaughterhouse."

"Escape? Pig? What are you talking about?" demanded a voice.

Blabitha suddenly appeared beside their table in the lunchroom.

Zora swallowed hard. Monica held her breath. The secret! Nobody could find out about the pigs. Especially not Blabitha!

Jeannie looked up from the table. "Gee, Tabitha, you're the last person we expected to see — or wanted to!"

"Very funny, Sawchuk. What was Brace Face here saying about a pig? A relative of yours, maybe?" Blabitha gave her sly smile.

Jeannie tossed back her braids. "Not that it's any of your business, but we were talking about—" she looked down and saw Super Pig's pointy ear sticking out of her backpack on the floor, "—we were talking about Super Pig. My toy."

"Awwwwwww. Do you always make up adventures about your little toys, Jeannie?" Blabitha said sweetly.

Jeannie fought down the urge to give Blabitha a good kick. Instead she said, "We're making up a story about Super Pig," her mind whirled, "for our junior kindergarten reading buddies. It's sort of like the three little pigs, but—"

"But they're sent to market—" Monica added quickly.

"And then they escape," Zora finished.

"Why Brace Face, that's adorable," sneered Blabitha.

Jeannie flushed. "Don't go away mad. Just go away!" she snapped.

"Yeah Tabitha," said Zora, "don't you have places to go and people to bother?"

"Yeah, you're one in a million, Tabitha. Thank heavens!" added Monica.

Blabitha made a face, then stalked away. The girls sighed with relief.

"Wow. That was close," said Monica. "I can't believe she bought that story." She glared at Tabitha surrounded by her friends on the other side of the room, and added, "Blabitha thinks she's so cool."

"Yeah. She thinks she's *all bad*, that's for sure," said Zora. Her voice changed. "I'm sorry I talked about the you-know-what. I didn't think anyone could hear us," she added humbly. She started to pick at her braces with a fingernail.

"That's okay," said Jeannie, "I didn't see her either."

"Yeah it's okay, Zora," Monica agreed. "Besides, we've just discovered Blabitha has a weak spot."

"We have?" asked Jeannie.

"Yeah," replied Monica, "It's right above her neck!"

The girls hooted with laughter.

Jeannie had a thought. "Let's call the mother pig Super Pig!" she said in a low voice. "Then nobody else will know what we're talking about."

"Great," whispered Zora back. "And we can call the other you-know-what, Super Piglet!"

Jeannie nodded.

"Well, has anyone got any ideas about Super Pig and Super Piglet?" asked Monica. "How are we going to save them?"

Zora and Jeannie shook their heads.

"We don't have much time left."

Jeannie glanced at the lunchroom clock.

"Speaking of time, I've got track practise now," she said gloomily. "I don't feel like going anymore, but I guess I'd better."

"While you're there, Monica and I can go to the library," said Zora. "Maybe we can find something there that will help out Super Pig."

"Yeah," laughed Monica, "we'll put our Girl Power into action by doing — *hamwork*!"

Jeannie smiled and gently stroked one of Super Pig's ears; ears that looked just like Mr. Spock's. "Well, live long and prosper," she said, giving them the Vulcan salute. "See you after track!"

CHAPTER SEVEN

The Hardest Part of Doing Nothing

That night Jeannie telephoned Granny O about the pigs.

"Are they still around?" Jeannie asked.

"Yes. This morning I saw the mother and the piglet on the edge of the woods.

"And have you girls come up with a plan yet? My lettuce is almost ready to plant out in the garden."

"Not really," said Jeannie. "Monica and Zora did some research on wild pigs in the school library. Most of the web sites on the Internet have to do with hunting pigs for sport. I guess it's big business in some parts of the world. They even do it from helicopters."

Granny O gave a snort of disgust. "How shooting animals from a helicopter can be considered sport, is beyond me."

"Zora said that in India, farmers beat on big drums to scare away the monkeys and the wild pigs."

Granny O laughed. "Well unless you girls want to beat on a drum day and night for a week, you better come up with a different plan.

"This Friday is Field Day, isn't it, Jeannie? Are you ready for your big race?"

Jeannie sadly told Granny O that girls her age could not compete in the 800-metre race. "It isn't fair," Jeannie continued. "Girls and boys should be treated the same."

"I agree, dear," said Granny O, "So what are you going to do about it?"

Jeannie was startled. "Nothing," she replied.

"Jeannie, the hardest part of doing nothing, is knowing when to stop. If you think it's unfair, don't just complain to me. Do something! Use your Girl Power!"

Jeannie just told her grandmother she had to go and do her homework now. It was all very well, Jeannie thought later, for an adult to say "do something!", but how could a kid change the way things were?

Friday turned out to be sunny and warm; perfect weather for the Mudcat Field Day. From her desk, Jeannie stared out the open window across the school playground. There were white blobs in the lawn where the dandelions had gone to seed.

Jeannie watched a gull drop out of the sky with a screech. It frantically began to poke away at something in the grass. There must be food over there, thought Jeannie.

With a scream, three more gulls landed in the grass and waddled up to the first bird. A noisy fight broke out as the first gull tried to drag its treasure away. Finally Jeannie saw what all the fuss was about. A dead fish! Someone must have thrown it on the playground as a joke. More and more gulls showed up until the grass was covered with hungry birds.

"Hey, what's going on out there?" one of the kids said. The teacher was out of the room and the class rushed over to the windows.

"The gulls are fighting over a fish," Jeannie reported.

"Well," said Ziggy, the class jokester, "you can tune a guitar, and you can tune a violin, but—"

Everyone else quickly chimed in, "—but you can't tune-a-fish!"

From the window they saw Mr. Hobbes, the janitor, come putt-putting around the corner of the school on his riding lawnmower. With one hand he steered toward the flock of gulls. In the other hand he carried a long, pointed stick.

A cheer went up from the classroom. "Our knight in shining armour has arrived!" shouted Ziggy.

Mr. Hobbes shook the stick angrily at the birds.

"Look! He's going to do battle with the Evil Gull Empire," laughed Monica. "Sir Hobbes of the Round Table is on his way to a joust!"

The gulls sullenly hopped out of the way of the riding mower and Mr. Hobbes speared the large fish with his stick. He wheeled the mower around and putt-putted toward the school dumpster.

"My hero," cried Zora, in a high, sugary voice, "on his trusty steed." She threw back her head and pretended to swoon. Monica gave Zora's ponytail a friendly tug.

"Hey, look!" said Jeannie. The gulls were furious at the loss of their fish. Now they wheeled above the mower, shrieking and screaming. The bolder birds dove angrily at Mr. Hobbes. He hunched miserably over the steering wheel but did not change his course. Occasionally he peered up at the sky, bracing himself for more attacks. Once he even shook the fish at his winged tormentors.

As the mower reached a large patch of

dandelions, clouds of the white fluffy dande-
lion seeds, churned up by the engine, swirled
around the janitor and his machine.

"Hey look! It's magic fairy dust!" laughed
Monica. "Maybe it will make the gulls vanish!"

But it didn't. The hungry, angry birds continued to circle and scream overhead.

Just then the class heard another noise above the sound of shrieking gulls.

BOOM-baba-BOOM-baba-BOOM.

Jeannie and the others saw the car full of teenagers cruise along Maple Avenue behind the playground. The car windows were rolled down and the stereo throbbed out a song.

"Looks like someone's skipping classes at Williamsville High," said Jeannie.

BOOM-baba-BOOM-baba-BOOM blared out into the soft, warm air. The gulls, shocked by the blast of violent sound, stopped fighting over the fish. Noisily they flew off toward the peace and quiet of the lake.

"Well, that's one way to scare off the local wildlife," laughed Ziggy.

"Speaking of wild life," Monica murmured to Zora.

The class watched Winston the Wookie trot across the playground to the track and field area. His furry arms were clutching piles of brightly-coloured first-, second- and third-place ribbons. As usual, his official "I am a coach" whistle dangled from his hairy neck. Beside him straggled someone small in a worn and faded tiger costume. The long tail drooped and the smiling tiger head completely covered the wearer's face.

Ms. Hampson came back into the room.

"Who has to be the Tiger Cat today?" Zora wondered aloud. Having to wear the hot, smelly old tiger cat costume was a J.J. Metcalf punishment. It was worse than ten detentions.

"Don't know," said Ms. Hampson. "Back to your seats now, class. It's almost time for Field Day to begin." She continued, "Remember, you won't be allowed back into school before lunch recess. So leave nothing behind. Nothing," she repeated firmly.

As Jeannie stuffed sun-block, a water bottle and Super Pig into her backpack, she remembered what Granny O had said about doing nothing. She knew girls were being treated unfairly. And she knew Coach Winston would never bother to complain to the Track and Field Association.

"Be a good girl and don't make a fuss," Winston the Wookie had told her. Well, Jeannie thought, if the mother pig had been a "good girl," she wouldn't have escaped. And she and her piglet would be dead.

Jeannie's eyes narrowed. She grabbed a pen and a pad of lined paper and tucked them into her backpack. It was time, she decided, to make a great, big fuss. But she couldn't do it alone.

CHAPTER EIGHT

Running For Her Life

"Go Jeannie! Go Jeannie!"

She could hear them screaming as she made her last lap around the track. There were two other runners just ahead of her; the rest of the runners followed far behind in a clump. As her legs pounded along, it was becoming harder and harder to catch her breath.

As Jeannie made the last turn around the track, she heard Monica and Zora scream above the crowd.

"Do it for Super Pig!" they shouted.

With the finish line in sight, Jeannie thought of Super Pig, running for her life. Running from a slaughterhouse death. Jeannie imagined that she too, was running for her life. That she was escaping from the slaughterhouse.

With that terrifying thought, new energy

rushed through her body. Jeannie suddenly felt herself surge forward. She was running faster than she had ever run before.

"Super Pig! Super Pig!" Jeannie could hear the shouts as she moved up past the lead runners.

"Super Pig! Super Pig!" Jeannie flew across the finish line. First! She had come in first!

Jeannie bent over double, gasping for breath, while Zora and Monica screamed and danced for joy. Monica ran up and handed her a water bottle.

"You did it, Jeannie. You did it. You won!"

Jeannie nodded and took a swallow of water. It felt wonderfully cool as it trickled down her throat. Still gasping, she squirted more water on her head and face. Zora handed her a towel and she wiped her face and neck.

There was an ear-piercing whine as Principal Allard turned the loudspeaker on to announce the winners of the race. He breathed heavily into the microphone held closely to his mouth.

"Atten-ssshun teachersssh and studentsssh. The firssshht and sssshecond place winnershhh in the 800-metre racesssh are Nicky Sssstavros and Fred Duval.

Zora and Monica frowned and shook their heads in disgust. No mention of Jeannie Sawchuk, the real winner.

"The next racesssh will be the girl'sssssh 400-metre racesssh. All girlsssssh running in the 400-metre dassshhh are to take their placesssshes at the sshhhtart line…Now!" There was another metallic whine followed by a loud clunk as Principal Allard switched the loudspeaker off.

"Come on, Jeannie," said Zora. "It's time for your next race." She took Jeannie's towel and water bottle away. "And no more water right now. It'll make you sick."

Zora and Monica steered Jeannie, who was still panting, over to the 400-metre start line.

Her lungs were hurting and her throat felt raw, but Jeannie automatically took the starting position. Blabitha, looking ice-cube cool, slipped into the space beside her.

Beads of sweat still formed on Jeannie's face and her shirt was plastered to her back.

Blabitha looked Jeannie up and down with a smirk. "Well, one thing is plain, Sawchuk — and that's you. A loser like you could never win this race."

"Yay Jeannie!" shouted Zora and Monica from the sidelines, but Jeannie knew it was hopeless. She was tired before the race even began.

"Go!" shouted the starter. Jeannie gave her best as she ran down the track and across the finish line. But it was no use. Blabitha came in first and one of her cool friends came in second. Jeannie finished fourth.

Monica ran up to the finish line, waving Jeannie's towel and water bottle.

"Nice try!" said Monica. "Way to go, Jeannie."

Jeannie had never felt so tired. She wiped the towel across her face and tried to get her breath. "I don't know," she gasped. Maybe, she thought as she took a gulp of water, this was all just a big waste of time. Maybe nobody else really cared that girls were being treated unfairly.

Jeannie tried not to feel bitter, as she eyed the admiring crowd around Blabitha. Nobody admired a fourth-place runner.

Monica handed Super Pig to Jeannie.

"Look at that Blabitha strutting around," she muttered. "You're the better runner.

"But don't worry, Jeannie, our Girl Power is about to swing into action. Zora," Monica added with a smile, "has a surprise."

CHAPTER NINE

This Story Has Legs

Zora appeared out of the crowd with a pretty young black woman carrying a large camera case.

"Jeannie, you remember my cousin Hassiba. She's going to be a TV newscaster one day," Zora said proudly. "But right now, she's a reporter with the *Williamsville Nugget*. I told her all about the race."

Hassiba smiled. "It's an interesting story angle. I'd like to do an article for the paper on what happened here today. But first I need to check the facts. Then I'll take pictures of Jeannie and Zora and — what's your name honey?"

"Monica."

"—of you and Zora and Monica," said Hassiba.

Blabitha pushed through the crowd that was forming around Hassiba Parks and the girls. "Why do you want Jeannie Sawchuk's picture?" complained Blabitha. "She didn't win anything today. *I'm* the winner. *I* won the 400-metre race."

"That's sweet, honey," Hassiba smoothly dismissed Blabitha with a wave of her hand, "but I have a nose for news. And this," she pointed at Jeannie, Monica and Zora, "is a true human interest story. As they say in the news business, this story has legs."

She turned back to the three girls and pulled out a small, battered notebook. "Now Zora has told me most of the story, but let me get this straight. You, Jeannie Sawchuk, ran in the 800-metre race, even though it was only for boys."

"That's right," said Monica, jumping in eagerly. "The rules said only boys could win the race. But the rules didn't say only boys could *run* in the race."

"We talked our homeroom teacher, Ms. Hampson, into letting Jeannie run the 800," said Zora. "She was in charge of that race."

"Really? I had Ms. Hampson when I went to school here," said Hassiba.

By now Jeannie had caught her breath. She added, "Ms. Hampson didn't think the rules were fair either."

"Okay, so you ran the race to show that

girls had the strength to run the 800. And you even won the race. But because you were a girl, you weren't given any award. Is that right?" asked Hassiba.

"Right," said Jeannie. "And I can't go on to the Regional Finals either."

"Jeannie won't tell you this," said Monica, "but because she had just finished running the 800-metre race, she was really tired when she ran the girls' 400. So she didn't win that race, but she should have!"

"Well," said Jeannie modestly, "we don't know that for sure."

"Yes we do," said Zora. "Jeannie gave up her chance to win the 400 when she ran the 800. She gave it up to prove her point!"

"Well," said Hassiba, as she wrote in her notebook, "we'll describe Jeannie as one of the favorites in today's 400."

She looked up. "And you girls also have a petition?"

Zora nodded and pulled Jeannie's notepad out of her backpack. It contained pages and pages of signatures. "That's right. Dad called the Track and Field Association for me. They said they would consider changing the rules for next year's races, *if* we got enough people to sign a petition."

Zora tapped the pages. "We have a lot of names here from the kids and the teachers and the parents who came to watch. Nobody refused to sign; everyone agrees that girls should have an 800-metre race too."

"All of the boys in our class have signed our petition," added Monica. "Lots of other kids too. Even Nicky and Fred, the boys who won the ribbons in the 800-metre race, signed."

"That's because they don't want Jeannie beating them every time they run," snickered Ziggy from the crowd.

"So who went around and got the signatures?" asked Hassiba.

"We did," said Monica. "Zora and I went all around the playground today. Actually," she tried to look earnest, "we just took our 'Anything is paw-sible' school motto to heart!"

Most Mudcat Kids thought the motto was a bit dumb, but Monica knew adults melted over all that rah rah kind of stuff.

"What a great quote!" exclaimed Hassiba, scribbling madly in her notebook. "The readers will love it.

"And what's this?" she asked. Jeannie was still holding on to Super Pig. Hassiba leaned forward and touched a pink, V-shaped hoof. "Cute!"

"Oh, this is Super Pig. She's for good luck," said Jeannie. "You know, like a mascot. I mean, J.J. Mudcat has the Tiger Cat mascot. So Super Pig was *my* mascot."

"And did she help in the 800?" asked Hassiba. "I understand you ran your fastest time ever today."

"Well, you *could* say Super Pig helped me win the 800." Jeannie couldn't tell a newspaper reporter that she had won by thinking about the Super Pig who lived in the woods. They couldn't tell even a nice reporter like Hassiba Parks about the pigs at Granny O's.

"Super Pig!" said Monica and Zora with wide smiles.

"Girl Power!" said Jeannie.

"It *is* a great girl power story," agreed Hassiba. "The *Nugget* will want to follow up on this story for sure." She raised one eyebrow. "It will be interesting to see if the Track and Field Association can move up out of the Dark Ages."

She held up the camera. "Okay, I'm going to take a picture of Zora and Monica holding up the petition. And Jeannie, you stand beside them and hold Super Pig.

"Zora, stop picking at your braces!"

Hassiba adjusted the camera lens then snapped a picture. "Great. Now, again." She took a few more shots then put the camera back into its case.

Ms. Hampson appeared out of the crowd and shook Hassiba's hand. "Hassiba Parks, star reporter! And one of my first students," she said fondly.

Hassiba smiled. "Hi, Ms. Hampson. You've got quite the students here." She nodded toward Jeannie, Zora and Monica.

Ms. Hampson looked at them proudly. "Yes I do. I think girls today are going to make a real difference in the world. Don't you?"

"Yes I do!" said Hassiba.

"Oh-oh. The kids are smacking the Tiger Cat around again," said Ms. Hampson, peering across the playground. "I better rescue our mascot before they pull his tail off! Bye Hassiba." She disappeared in the crowd.

Hassiba checked her watch. "Oops, I've gotta go, too. I've got another story to cover. Bye girls!"

Hassiba began to hurry off, then stopped and called back over her shoulder. "Look for the story in next week's *Nugget*!" Then she rushed away.

Blabitha stalked over to the three girls. "That reporter only took your picture because she's related to Zora," she hissed. "She should have taken a picture of the winners, like me. Not of a bunch of losers, like you."

Jeannie decided it was time to set Blabitha straight.

"So, Tabitha," asked Jeannie, "how do you keep a loser in suspense?"

Blabitha narrowed her eyes. "I don't know," she said suspiciously.

Jeannie smiled wickedly and said, "I'll tell you next week."

CHAPTER TEN

It's So Crazy

The next day, Saturday, was another beautiful day. Once again Jeannie, Zora and Monica rode their bikes out to the Olafson farm.

When they arrived, the girls sat under a tree with Granny O and ate freshly baked chocolate chip cookies.

"I'm proud of the way you girls are working to change the rules." Granny O passed the plate of cookies around again. "Do you think the Track and Field Association will add an 800-metre race for girls?"

Zora nodded. "I think they will when they see all those names on our petition."

"And Hassiba's article will help too," added Monica. She carefully brushed a cookie crumb off her T-shirt. "It'll be in next week's paper, so we'll put a copy in with the petition."

"My dad will make sure it gets to the right people at the Track and Field Association office," added Zora.

Jeannie stopped munching her cookie and pointed toward the woods. "There they are!"

They looked over and saw Super Pig and Super Piglet at the edge of the wood.

"They're getting bolder and bolder," said Granny O. She sounded annoyed, but Jeannie could tell that, deep down, her grandmother liked the pigs as much as the girls did.

"I think Super Piglet has grown since last week," Jeannie added.

Zora nodded. "The library book said that in the wild, pigs eat acorns, mushrooms, roots — all sorts of things like that. They can eat almost anything."

"Well, there are lots of things for them to eat around here," said Granny O. "The oak wood, of course, is full of acorns. And Crooked Creek runs through those woods, so there's lots of drinking water."

She made a face. "But those bad pigs had better stay away from my garden."

Granny O got to her feet and picked up the cookie plate. "I checked again with Cortino's Hardware. I won't be able to buy any posts or fencing wire for another week.

So girls, it's time for you to put your plan into action." She shook her head. "It's so crazy that it just might work."

She handed her portable cassette player to Jeannie. "It's a waterproof case, and I've put in new, long-life batteries. Now if you'll excuse me girls, I've got work to do."

Jeannie rummaged through her backpack and pulled out some cassettes. She picked one and slipped it into the cassette player.

"Are you sure your brother won't mind you taking his tapes?" asked Monica anxiously.

Jeannie shook her head. "Naw. He's into compact discs now. Rudy won't even notice these tapes are gone."

The three girls walked out to Granny O's vegetable garden and placed the cassette player between the garden and the oak wood. The pigs, who had wandered out into the meadow, watched their every move.

Jeannie admired their attitude. They boldly go where no pig has ever gone before, she told herself with a smile.

"Sorry pigs," said Zora with a grin, "but you've been bad to the bone. So this is for your own good."

Jeannie turned the volume control on high, pushed the cassette's play button, and stepped back.

BOOM-baba-BOOM-baba-BOOM vibrated across the meadow toward the woods as the heavy metal band screamed out its first song.

Super Pig and Super Piglet, shocked by the brutal noise, jumped in terror. They spun around and fled across the meadow. The bushes shook as they vanished into the oak wood. Those pigs really can run, thought Jeannie.

All three girls stuck their fingers in their ears to block out the painful sounds.

"You were right, Zora," shouted Monica above the noise. "It sounds like someone's beating a drum."

Zora nodded and shouted back, "And grinding up car parts at the same time. Let's go! It's making my braces vibrate!"

"Now you know why they call these things 'boom boxes'," Jeannie shouted.

The three girls hurried back to Granny O's house.

It was peaceful there, although there was still a faint throb of music in the air. Jeannie pulled Super Pig from her backpack and stroked her Vulcan ears.

Granny O appeared with a plastic tray full of tiny green plants. "Time to set out my next crop of lettuce," she said with a smile. "But

I'll shut that noise off when I'm out there."

"Oh, I almost forgot!" said Monica, reaching into a pocket. "The Olafson Oak! Here are the pictures I took for our project. They're great!"

Granny O and Zora crowded around Monica to admire her photographs.

Jeannie quietly slipped away from the others. She gazed across the meadow at the distant woods and smiled. Knowing that the pigs still ran free filled her with a deep, fierce joy.

Jeannie gave Super Pig a hug, then slowly held her own hand up in the V-shaped Vulcan salute. "Live long and prosper, little pigs," she murmured, "Live long and prosper!"

THE END

About the Author

Born and raised in London, Ontario, Susan Merritt received her BA in English and her law degree from the University of Western Ontario. She is the author of the award winning *Her Story* and *Her Story II: Women from Canada's Past. The Stone Orchard*, her young adult novel, was shortlisted for the Geoffrey Bilson Award for historical fiction. Her first Mudcat Kids series chapter books, *Cheddar* and *Down in the Dumpster*, are winners of the Canadian Children's Book Centre 'Our Choice' Award. Susan lives in Ridgeway, Ontario with her husband and two children.